DO NOT
Go Down
The Wrong Street

ISBN: Softcover 978-1-6698-1536-5
eBook 978-1-6698-1537-2

Print information available on the last page.

Rev. date: 04/14/2022

To order additional copies of this book, contact:
Xlibris
844-714-8691
www.Xlibris.com
Orders@Xlibris.com
832582

This book is dedicated to my great-nieces and great-nephews whom I love dearly. Remember that you can change the world one good deed at a time. *Responsibility, Citizenship, Kindness, Respect, Honesty, Self-Control, Tolerance,* and *Cooperation* are the cornerstones of your growth and development. You will be judged by your actions, your character matters!

Mom and Grandma are always talking about not going down the wrong street. Anytime my sister's and I get in trouble we hear some type of story about going down the wrong street. I decided to keep my own personal journal about going down the wrong street. I even wrote some stories of my own about going down the wrong street.

You see, going down the wrong street can take you very far away from where you live. The things that you encounter on these unfamiliar streets never seem to have any positive outcomes or results. Going down the wrong street may be the reason why my dad is not here for me to share the things I have in my journal.

My first going down the wrong street speech happened when my teacher called my house. I decided to join a group of classmates who always get in trouble during the school day. Well, I really do not know what made me decide to join them in disrupting our teacher's instruction; but I did. I probably felt that it would be cool, and I could make my classmates laugh. Nothing was funny when mom called me to the kitchen as she spoke to my teacher on the telephone.

Have you ever received a negative phone call from a teacher? Please share what happened in the space provided:

Her facial expressions said it all; I was in trouble. Mom never was the one to rush and spank any of us, but her "going down the wrong street" talks would sting your soul. She started with: have I not told you about RESPECT? DO YOU NOT KNOW WHAT IT MEANS? Of course, my short answer to each of her questions were "yes ma'am. Then came the part about how hard she works every day to make sure that my sisters and I have everything we need. The only thing she asked us to do is go to school, do the best we can do, and always be respectful to our teachers. Anything other than that would lead us to "going down the wrong street."

Lesson learned here: You do not have to try and fit in with the crowd by doing things that go against your positive upbringing. Do not disrespect anyone to gain popularity amongst your peers. Treat your teachers the way you want to be treated.

As I headed to school the next day, my mom's words played over and over in my head. I certainly was not going to go down the wrong street today. I do not quite have the confidence to tell my friends that they are going down the wrong street; but I certainly will do my best not to join them again. I refused to let their negative behavior pull me in again.

Mom apologized to my teacher during that telephone conversation, and I was certain that she was going to tell me to do the same. Somehow, she never got around to doing that. Perhaps she was tired from work or just too disappointed about my behavior. As soon as I entered the classroom, I was overwhelmed with the feeling that I needed to apologize to her. I started practicing over and over in my head what I was going to say. I even started thinking about what my friends would say if they saw me apologizing to our teacher. I immediately panicked because I was afraid not being a cool kid. But wait! Does being cool mean that I must be disrespectful? Should I go against what mom and grandma have taught me? Hmmm, I sat there thinking about that for a long time. No, being cool is not worth failing to respect my teacher. I am going to raise my hand, ask to come to her desk and I am going to apologize for my behavior on yesterday. I raised my hand and she asked, "may I help you"? I asked to come up to her desk and she replied yes. Of course, my classmates were all watching as I walked towards her desk. My nerves were wrecked but I was confident about what I was going to say to her.

Nothing fancy filled with a lot of words. I simply said, "Mrs. Blue I am very sorry about my behavior yesterday." Mrs. Blue stated that she was taken by surprised when I behaved disrespectfully yesterday. She accepted my apology and stated that she does not expect that to ever happened again. Once she said that a big feeling of relief passed through my little body. As I walked backed to my seat, I felt different. I felt great! When I finished my assignment, I pulled out my journal, opened my dictionary and looked up the word RESPECT. Mom and grandma had given me their version of Respect, but I wanted to add the definition of Respect to my journal.

RESPECT is: Showing consideration, understanding, and regard for people, places, and things.

What does respect look like to you?

I guess Mom shared the telephone conference she had with my teacher with my grandma. One day she knocked on my bedroom door and I was surprised that Grandma had come for a visit. We did are usual hug and kisses. She asked me how I was doing and how things were going at school. Back in her day she said the focus would be Reading, Writing, and Arithmetic! She would tell us that discipline was not a problem because Negro boys and girls understood the importance of respect and getting an education. At that time many of them would eventually be responsible for teaching their parents how to read. Grandma sort of eased her way into getting on me about my disrespectful behavior. I told her that I thought it would make me a little more popular with my classmates. Boy was I wrong! I also told her that I decided to apologize to Mrs. Blue on my own and that I felt great afterwards. Grandma told me that she was proud of me and that I had demonstrated a form of **"INTEGRITY".** Integrity I asked? Yes, she stated, the fact that I had decided to apologize without anyone telling me to do so was indeed a form of integrity. Now that made me feel better than any of my friends or classmates ever have! My journal vocabulary list is starting to grow. All sorts of words will probably fill my "Do Not Go Down the Wrong Street" Journal by the time I reach Middle School.

***O**ther than your parents, who are some trusted adults that you feel comfortable sharing your thoughts and feelings? Why?*

I have several years to go before I go to Middle School. Two of my sisters are in Middle School and the oldest is in High School. Most times they make me leave their room when they are talking about school, friends, and other things that they say I am too young to hear. Sometimes I can hide under a bed or in their closet and ease drop on some of their conversations.

Whew, I am sure glad that I am considered a little kid! Their days are filled with encounters of going down the wrong street. How do they manage to handle these encounters and school at the same time? How are they able to avoid going down the wrong street? Will I be able to be like them when I attend middle and high school? Now I am sure that I have violated some type of rule by hiding under the bed and in the closet. But it is worth any punishment I may receive because I am learning a lot. Most of all I am proud of my big sisters. They really are listening to Mom and Grandma. Each of them is taking Mom and Grandma little talks very seriously. I picked up on three words that were familiar to me during my ease dropping. They were ***HONESTY, RESPONSIBILITY, AND SELF-CONTROL.***

My sister Pamela is always so truthful, she is the first one to tell exactly what happened when Mom or Grandma say, "don't lie to me." So, in my journal I drew a picture of Pamela next to HONESTY.

Which Character Education Traits describe one or more of your siblings?

HONESTY is being truthful, trustworthy, and sincere. Yep, that is my sister Pamela! Trustworthy and Sincere; she is the one I tell all my secrets to. My oldest sister Alesia is the responsible one. My mom has given her a lot of responsibilities as our big sister. She sometimes thinks that she is my mother and I tell her that she is not. I do not get carried away with that comment; I just feel like saying that to her sometimes. I guess it is part of me growing up and maturing. No matter how I react to her, she lets me know that she is accountable for me when Mom is not around. ***RESPONSIBILITY*** is meeting obligations by being reliable, accountable, and dependable to self and others. ***SELF-CONTROL*** is having discipline over one's behavior and actions. My sister Fredi talked about how she refuses to respond with anger to a situation involving a girl in her class. Seems as if this girl is having a problem with demonstrating self-control. She is loud, bullying, and always giving an excuse for her behavior. Fredi, though she is not the oldest; she is indeed the one who does not fear anything. So, for her to talk about self-control, I know that I can do the same. I also remembered that Mrs. Blue (my teacher) was big on teaching us ***TOLERANCE.*** Tolerance is recognizing and respecting differences, values, and beliefs of other people. She always says that if we did that the world would be a better place and school would be enjoyable for all!

I oftentimes wonder if our dad or grandfather had any "DO NOT GO DOWN THE WRONG STREET" advice. Mom does not talk about dad very much. When she does it is never anything negative. She would just say little things like: "your dad would want the best for you, or your dad would be proud of you." ***There have been a few times when I overheard Grandma and her talking about praying that I do not make the same mistakes Dad did.*** I wonder what those mistakes were. I guess I will have to wait until they are ready to tell me. Probably has something to do with going down the wrong street.

Our Grandfather died when our mother was in high school. She tells us stories about him and how great he was. No one knows it but I also have things in my journal about my grandfather. Two words that have been constant when describing my grandfather are ***KINDNESS*** AND ***CITIZENSHIP.*** He was very kind to his family and friends. He served his Country in the United States Army; and he never violated any rules or regulations that caused him to be considered a criminal. Mrs. Blue introduced us to Eight Character Education Traits earlier in the school year. So, I recognized ***Kindness*** and ***Citizenship*** immediately. I thought about the picture of my grandfather with him in his army uniform covered with ribbons and medals.

I am sure that all of them were earned because of his character. ***KINDNESS*** is being helpful, thoughtful, caring, compassionate, and considerate. ***CITIZENSHIP*** is knowing, understanding, and displaying high regard for the rules, laws, government, heritage, and those who have served and sacrificed for community and country. Anytime I finish my work early in class, I enjoy flipping through the pages of my journal. It excites me to know that my grandfather was a great man! It also feels great to know that my sisters and I are being taught things that are so important no matter where we go.

Unfortunately, that joy goes away when I wonder if my dad had people who told him not to go down the wrong street when he was my age. Did he know about the Eight Character Education Traits? Is that the reason why he is not here to help Mom and Grandma raise me and my sisters? I have so many questions in my little head. But I will continue to write these thoughts in my journal and one day I will have the answers! The most important thing I am going to focus on is not going down the wrong street that may cause me to not demonstrate **CITIZENSHIP, COOPERATION, HONESTY, INTEGRITY, KINDNESS, RESPECT, SELF-CONTROL, AND TOLERANCE.** I am going to make sure that I always practice these traits throughout elementary, middle, and high school. I am certain that if I do, I will not "go down the wrong street" mom and grandma warned me about.

Oh no, Mom is calling me! If I answer her, my sisters will realize that I am hiding under the bed ease dropping on their conversations! Always remember not to go down the wrong street!

Reader Engagement

Going Down the Wrong Street is told by nine-year-old Mari. He and his three sisters are being raised by a single mother. His grandmother also plays a major role in his upbringing. Create a journal of your own and share your thoughts about the following questions:

1. Why is it important to demonstrate Respect?

2. The best way to remember the Eight Character Education Traits is to place them in alphabetical order. Please write them in that order.

3. With whom do you share your secrets? Why them?

4. Which of the Eight Character Education Traits do you like? Why?

5. Why do you think Mari's mom and grandmother pray that he does not make the same mistakes as his dad?

Reader Engagement

Reader's Journal